Word List

Here is a list of words that might make it easier to read this book. You'll find them in boldface the first time they appear in the story.

championship	CHAM-pee-uhn-ship
uniforms	YOO-nuh-forms
jerseys	JER-zees
referee	re-fuh-REE
interviewing	IN-ter-vyoo-ing
salami	sul-LO-mee
contact	KON-takt
exhausted	ig-ZAWS-tid
laundry	LAWN-dree
Foul	fowl
forfeit	FOR-fuht
confession	kuhn-FE-shun
officials	uh-FI-shuls
pulverize	PUHL-vuh-reyez

Barbie™

Double Trouble

BARBIE and associated trademarks are owned by and used under
license from Mattel, Inc. © 2000 Mattel, Inc. All Rights Reserved.
Published by Grolier Books, a division of Grolier Enterprises, Inc.
Story by Della Foster and Linda Williams Aber.
Photo crew: James Atiee, Shirley Ushirogata, Dave Bateman, Patrick Kittel,
Michael Corona, Susan Cracraft, Lisa Collins, and Judy Tsuno.
Produced by Bumpy Slide Books.
Printed in the United States of America.
ISBN: 0-7172-8960-5

GROLIER
B O O K S

The score was tied with fifteen seconds left in the game. The Pro Women's Basketball **championship** could go to either team.

From the sidelines, eleven-year-old Jen Martinez stared at the court. "Girls!" a man called over the noise of the crowd. "Watch how the Rockets move into position after the time-out." Jen wasn't really listening. Her eyes never left the women in blue **uniforms.** Their **jerseys** matched the one Jen was wearing. The Rockets were her favorite team. Number eleven, Barbie Roberts, was her favorite player.

A horn sounded. The two-minute time-out was over. The crowd jumped to its feet as the two teams raced back onto the court. The **referee** blew a sharp blast on her whistle.

All the players moved at once. The ball looked like an orange blur as it flew from player to player. A dark-haired woman in a blue uniform caught the ball. But before she could take a step, two women in red uniforms surrounded her. Ten seconds were left.

Suddenly a tall, blond woman in blue pulled away from her guard. Her dark-haired teammate passed her the ball.

"Barbie's got the ball!" Jen shouted. Five seconds were left.

Barbie ran past a guard on the Wildcats and shot. The ball sailed into the air.

SWISH! It was good. The crowd roared! The buzzer sounded. The game was over.

"We won!" Jen shouted.

On the court, the Rockets were cheering and hugging one another. Cameras flashed as reporters surrounded the players.

Jen turned to her own teammates. "That's going to be us on Friday!" she declared.

"If we're lucky," a red-haired girl named Debbie answered.

"Luck doesn't have much to do with it, girls," Coach Curtis said. He had brought Jen's basketball team to the game as a treat. "It's hard work that counts," the coach explained. "And because you've been working so hard all season, I have a surprise for you."

"A surprise?" the girls shouted at once.

"The reporters are **interviewing** the players now," the smiling coach said. "But when they're done, you can meet my friend Barbie."

"Barbie Roberts is your *friend?*" gasped a girl named Paulina with short, black hair.

Coach Curtis nodded. "Ever since she

played for the women's team at my college."

"Will she sign our programs?" Debbie asked.

"Sure," Coach Curtis replied. "Let's go."

"Oh! This is going to be so cool!" Jen exclaimed. They grabbed their programs and followed their coach through the crowd.

"I can't believe your twin sister didn't want to come," Paulina said to Jen. "She's the only one from our team who's not here."

"I know," Jen agreed. "I tried to talk her into coming. But she was too busy working on her science project." She sighed. "You know my sister. She'd rather study than watch a basketball game. Even a game as exciting as this one."

"That's so strange," Debbie said, shaking her head. "You and Cindy are twins. But you're total opposites. You're messy and love sports. Cindy's neat and loves getting *A*'s."

"Hey, I get *A*'s, too!" Jen argued.

"Yeah?" Paulina chimed in. "In what?"

4

"Gym," Jen replied shyly. "Cindy's always had it easier when it comes to school."

"Okay, team!" Coach Curtis called. "Here we are." They had reached a door with a sign that read *Sports Arena Staff Only.*

He showed a pass to the guard. The guard studied it for a moment, then waved them through.

"Thanks!" Coach Curtis said. He led the girls down a long hallway into a large room. Reporters and photographers were asking questions and taking pictures of the winning team.

"There she is!" Jen gasped. "It's Barbie Roberts!" The young player tried to comb her long, tangled hair with her fingers. But it was no use.

A reporter was finishing her interview. "Late in the game, the team looked to you for direction. How did you feel?" the reporter asked Barbie.

Barbie answered, "I really felt the pressure. But I knew if we worked hard, and worked together, we would win."

When the reporter had finished, Barbie turned to her friend. "Kevin!" she exclaimed. "Has your wife had the baby yet?"

"Not yet," Coach Curtis replied, "but soon. She didn't feel up to coming. You played a really great game. Congratulations!"

"Thanks," said Barbie. "It's a great way to end a season!" She smiled at the girls standing next to Kevin. "And you must be the Garden City Gators. I hear you have your final game of the season coming up, too," she added.

The girls just stood with their mouths open.

Coach Curtis chuckled at his starstruck team. "Yes, our team is tied for first place with the Peekskill Puffins," he answered for them.

Finally Jen blurted out, "Barbie, would you sign my program? Please?"

"Mine, too!" the other girls shouted.

"Sure," Barbie said, taking Jen's program. "I'd love to see you girls play sometime."

"We have practice tomorrow," the excited girl quickly offered.

"Barbie's probably busy," Coach Curtis began.

"Actually," Barbie said with a grin, "I'd enjoy coming. That is, if it's all right with your coach."

All eyes turned to Coach Curtis. "Please, please, *please?*" the girls begged.

Coach Curtis laughed. "Okay, I could use the coaching help. But if you want to win Friday's game, we're going to have to work hard."

Jen nodded. "We will!"

All the way home, the team talked happily.

"Won't it be terrific?" Jen said. "On Monday we'll practice with a pro basketball player. And on Friday, the Gators will stuff the Puffins in the finals. This is going to be a great week!"

Chapter Two

At school the next day, the basketball team met in the lunchroom. By the time Jen arrived, everyone was almost finished eating.

Her friend Debbie shook her head. "Here comes Jen. Late, as usual."

"I couldn't find my lunch," Jen explained. "But it was in my locker under my sneakers."

The other girls groaned.

Jen just shrugged and sat down next to her sister, who wore glasses. Otherwise, the two girls looked exactly alike. "Did Mom give you anything good today, Cindy?" Jen stuck her nose into her twin sister's bag. "Yuck! Smells like fish!"

Cindy yanked her lunch back from her sister. "It's tuna!" she said. "Besides, it smells better than your sneakers." Cindy watched as her twin began placing potato chips on her sandwich. "*Another* **salami**-and-potato-chip sandwich?" she asked.

Jen took a big, crunchy bite. "It's the lunch of champions!" Chips fell out of her mouth as she spoke. "I'll bet Barbie would love one of these!"

Cindy handed her sister a napkin. "Yeah. And *I'll* be chosen most valuable player of the season."

The other girls giggled. Even though Cindy was on the team, it was Jen who was their star player.

"Do you really think Barbie will come to practice?" Debbie wondered.

"I doubt it," Cindy answered, pushing her glasses up on her nose. "Why would someone like Barbie come to *our* practice?"

"She will," Jen insisted, frowning at her twin. "I'm telling you: Eat like a champion, practice with a champion, *become* a champion."

"I don't know," Paulina said slowly. "We lost to the Puffins last time we played them."

"But only by two points," Debbie pointed out. "Besides, we have Jen."

"Not if she doesn't get her math homework done," warned her twin.

Jen gasped. "Uh-oh. I knew I forgot something." Just then the bell rang. The girls gathered their things and left for class.

After school Cindy did some homework in the library. She left early for practice. The squeaking of her sneakers echoed loudly in the quiet gym. She grabbed a basketball and stood behind the free throw line. *THUMP-THUMP.* Cindy bounced the ball, then shot. *BAM. SWISH.* The ball hit the backboard and went through the net. She got the ball and shot again.

Cindy was so busy practicing free throws she didn't notice someone watching her.

"That's great!" a woman's voice called.

Startled, Cindy spun around. She fixed her glasses and recognized Barbie from her sister's sports magazines.

"Hi!" Barbie said. "I remember you."

"You do?" Cindy asked, confused.

"Sure I do," Barbie replied. "I never forget a face. Your coach told me what a great player you are. Nice shooting, by the way."

Cindy's eyes widened in surprise. "Thanks," she replied, blushing. "I don't usually shoot very well with people watching," she said shyly.

Barbie laughed. "I get nervous, too. That's why practice is important. Arriving early for extra practice is the sign of a real champion," Barbie told her.

Cindy's smile grew. She had never been called that before, but she really liked it.

The gym door opened. Another girl with curly, brown hair entered. She wore a striped shirt and pants. "Early again, sis?" called Jen.

Barbie looked from one girl to the other. "Wait a minute," she said. "I'm seeing double." She looked at Cindy, in glasses, holding a ball. "If you're the basketball player I met last night, then who is this?" she asked, pointing to Jen.

Cindy's smile disappeared. She realized Barbie's mistake. "You may never forget a face," she said sadly. "But it's my *twin sister's* face you're remembering. It was Jen you met. I'm Cindy."

Barbie chuckled. "You sure fooled me. So Cindy's the one with glasses?"

"Right," Cindy replied. "I have **contact** lenses, too, but I never wear them. Jen wears hers all the time. Plus, Jen's the *real* basketball player."

"She's not the only one from what I just saw," Barbie said. Cindy's smile returned.

Soon the rest of the team arrived. Barbie told them, "Coach Curtis called me from the hospital. His wife had a baby girl. He asked me to fill in for

him until he returns."

The girls were thrilled and started asking questions. Barbie shared the details and added, "It's exciting. But we have to keep up the practice schedule. We want to beat the Puffins, right?"

"Right!" all the girls shouted.

Barbie didn't waste any time. "All right," she said. "Let's go through the warm-ups. They're just as important as playing games."

After warm-ups came the practice drills. Soon it was easy for Barbie to tell the twins apart. Jen breezed through each of the drills. Cindy had a harder time. In fact, she missed all the shots she tried.

Later, Barbie divided the girls into two teams for a short practice game. Barbie noticed that the girls on Jen's team were always passing her the ball. They did it even when they could take an easy shot themselves. The girls on Cindy's team almost never passed Cindy the ball. So she just jogged around, looking bored.

When practice was over, Barbie gathered the team together. "I've been watching everyone closely. Remember, no one person can win a game. To win, you have to depend on every player. That's what being a team is all about. Please think about that." Then Barbie added, "See you on Wednesday."

On their way home, the twins thought about what Barbie had said. Her words made sense. Both girls were happy to hear them for different reasons.

After dinner the twins lay on their bunk beds in the room they shared. Cindy was reading books for her science project on her bottom bunk. Jen was lying down on her top bunk, flipping through a sports magazine.

Cindy began, "You should think about your science project. You want to get an *A*, don't you?"

"What's so great about getting *A*'s?" Jen

asked. "All I can think about is Friday's game."

Cindy laughed. "If that were all I had to think about, I would feel lucky."

Jen shrugged and said, "Just do something easy for science, like me. I'm getting two plants. I'll water one more than the other. Then I'll see which one grows the most—piece of cake!"

"I can't do something that simple," Cindy told her. "I want to do something great and get an A. You don't know how hard that is. All you worry about is getting the ball in the basket. *That's* a piece of cake."

"Ha!" Jen exclaimed. "There's nothing easy about having a whole team counting on me to win. You're the one who has it easy."

"Yeah, sure. I'd switch places with you in a second," Cindy declared.

"I dare you!" Jen challenged. "Then we'd find out who has it easy and who doesn't."

"Some dare," Cindy shot back. "We could

never get away with it."

Jen sat up on her bed. "Wait, I'm serious!" she said, hopping down from the top bunk. "We've done it before. Remember in third grade? You switched places with me when I couldn't remember my lines in the class play. We fooled everyone!"

"We were younger," Cindy pointed out. "It was easier then."

Jen laughed. "Well, it would be easy for me. I'd just walk around with my nose in a book."

Cindy jumped to her feet. "It would be harder to be me than to be you. I'd just have to bounce a ball!"

"That's it," Jen said. "I challenge you to live my life for one day."

"I accept!" Cindy declared.

The twins shook hands. "Now you'll see how hard it is to be me!" both girls said at exactly the same time. Then they burst out laughing.

Neither twin could wait to prove herself right.

Chapter Three

"Good morning, *Jen,*" Jen sang out the next day. She hopped down from her bunk and stumbled to the bathroom to put in her contacts.

"Good morning, *Cindy,*" Cindy giggled. She grabbed her glasses from the nightstand.

"So far, so good," Jen called.

"But let's not switch until we're at school. We could never fool Mom and Dad," Cindy added.

"You're right," Jen agreed, walking back to their room. "We can change in the bathroom before school starts." She picked up a pair of ripped jeans and a wrinkled shirt from the floor.

"I think I would wear this today," she said.

"Ew!" Cindy cried, staring at the clothes.

"They're clean!" Jen promised. She smelled the shirt just to make sure.

Cindy sighed and walked to the closet. She pulled out a neatly ironed dress. "Well, I would wear this."

Jen groaned, "Aw! Do I have to?"

Her twin laughed. "You made the challenge. You wear the clothes."

When the girls got to school, they switched clothes in the bathroom. Jen put on glasses and tried to comb her hair neatly like Cindy's. Cindy put in her contacts, then messed up her hair like Jen's. Neither girl was very happy with her new "look."

Just then their friend Paulina walked in. "Hey, girls," she called. She checked her short, dark hair in the mirror. Then she turned to Jen. "Ready to read your poem today, Cindy?"

Cindy started to answer. But her sister stepped

on her foot to keep her from talking.

Cindy yelped anyway.

"Sorry," Jen apologized. Then she turned to Paulina and replied, "What poem?"

"The one I saw you with last night," Cindy reminded her, rubbing her foot.

Jen's jaw dropped. Cindy had given her a poem the night before to read for class. But the forgetful twin had left it on the kitchen table.

Cindy could see her sister's panic. "You didn't forget it, did you, Cindy?" she asked Jen.

"Uh, well . . ." Jen stammered.

Paulina laughed. "Cindy's a brain. She would never forget schoolwork. Especially since she's reading it in front of the whole class today."

"Right, I'm Cindy. I never forget anything," Jen reminded herself. "See you later, *Jen.*"

Cindy glared at her twin. "Good luck, *Cindy!*"

Paulina gave both sisters a puzzled look.

Then she and Jen left for English class.

Jen sat in the front of the room, as Cindy always did. The girl sitting behind her tugged gently on her hair. "Can I see your social studies notes?" the girl whispered.

"Yeah, me, too," the boy next to her added.

Jen was confused. Why would anyone want *her* notes? She took lousy notes. Then she realized they thought she was Cindy. Jen decided that she would need her sister's notes, too. "Sorry," she answered truthfully, "Jen needs them."

Then their English teacher, Mrs. Kirk, spoke. "We'll start this morning by finishing up our class poetry projects. Cindy, you can begin by reading us the poem you wrote. Please come up."

Jen gulped as all eyes in the class turned toward her. "Um," she sputtered, thumbing through some papers. "Just give me a minute to find it, Mrs. Kirk." Jen tried to think of all the rhyming words she knew. "Cat. Hat. Ball. Tall. Red. *Dead!*"

"Did you find it, Cindy?" Mrs. Kirk asked.

"Never fear. It's right here," Jen replied, still thinking of rhymes. The class giggled. Jen's face turned bright red.

"Very funny, Cindy," Mrs. Kirk said. "Ready?"

Jen finally grabbed a piece of paper. It was her math homework. "Here goes nothing," she thought. She walked slowly to the front of the classroom and stared at her math problems.

Mrs. Kirk looked at her and smiled. "Don't be nervous. I'm sure your poem is wonderful."

Jen shook her head. She was ready to confess everything. Her hands began to sweat. Her heart beat as fast as if she were playing basketball. Then she thought, "Basketball! That's it!" She cleared her throat and said, "My poem is called, 'I Love Basketball.'" She pretended to read out loud:

"How I love basketball.
It's really, uh, cool.
I like it much better
Than being in, um, school."

Jen looked up and smiled proudly. She waited for applause, but silence filled the room. Then a girl in the back row began to laugh. Soon the whole class was laughing at Jen's poem. Jen blushed and sat back down.

"That's enough, class," Mrs. Kirk scolded. "Thank you, Cindy. That was very—interesting."

After class Mrs. Kirk stopped Jen on her way out. "Cindy," she began, "could you please stay after class for a few minutes?"

"Sure, Mrs. Kirk," Jen replied with a sigh.

At lunch that day, Jen rushed into the cafeteria after the bell had rung. Cindy was already sitting with their friends Debbie and Paulina.

Debbie looked at Cindy, seated at the table with messy hair and clothes. Then she looked at Jen, standing in a dress and glasses. *"Cindy* is late?" she said, pointing at Jen. "Now that's a *switch!"*

The sisters tried not to giggle. Then Jen nodded at Cindy. "She must be rubbing off on me." When she opened her lunch bag, Jen caught a whiff of her sandwich. "Tuna!" she gasped.

Cindy covered a laugh and smiled wickedly. "You love that smelly fish, Cindy," she told Jen.

Jen frowned, then smiled a wicked grin of her own. "Well, I hope Mom sent your chips," she said. "Our star can't miss a day of salami-and-potato-chip sandwiches before the big game."

Cindy's face sank. She realized she had no choice. To be Jen, Cindy had to mess up her hair, wear dirty clothes, *and* eat the awful sandwich. So she stuffed her sandwich full of chips and took a big, crunchy bite. Potato chips fell everywhere.

Jen smiled and handed Cindy a napkin.

"So how did your poem go?" Cindy asked her twin suddenly.

"Uh," Jen stammered, "Mrs. Kirk liked it."

"Really?" Cindy asked. She could tell her sister was trying to hide something. "I have to go to the bathroom. Cindy, do you want to come?"

Before Jen could answer, Cindy dragged her away from the table. Once they were safe in the bathroom, Jen explained what had happened.

"It's not fair," Jen complained. "I thought my poem was good. But Mrs. Kirk gave me a *D!*"

Cindy's face burned with anger. "No! Mrs. Kirk gave *me* a *D*. She thinks you're me, remember?"

"Oh, that's right!" Jen said, smiling. "Then it isn't so bad."

Cindy stomped her foot. "Of course it's bad! I've never gotten a *D*."

"I'm really sorry," Jen began.

"I never should have let you talk me into this," Cindy snapped. "I should have known you would mess up my grades!"

"Then call it off," Jen challenged. "Tell Mrs. Kirk everything. Besides, you won't be able to make it through basketball practice, anyway."

"Says who?" Cindy blurted out. "Just watch me!" Then she stormed out of the bathroom.

Chapter Four

That afternoon Barbie was running practice again. "Okay," she said to the twins, "today I'm going to get your names right!" She looked at the twin wearing glasses. "You're Cindy," she said to Jen. "And you're Jen," she said to Cindy.

The sisters gave Barbie two thumbs up.

Barbie went through the warm-ups and stretches with the team. Then she announced, "Because this is our last practice, we're going to skip drills today. We'll go straight to a practice game."

Barbie divided the girls into two teams.

Cindy and Jen were again on opposite sides. From the beginning, Cindy noticed something. Because her teammates thought she was Jen, they passed the ball to her—a lot. At first, Cindy was thrilled. She even made a few baskets. But she soon got tired of it.

Once when Cindy turned around for a second, Debbie passed her the ball. *WHAP!* The ball whacked Cindy in the back. *THUD!* She fell facedown on the floor. Barbie blew her whistle and ran onto the court.

"Jen, are you okay?" Debbie asked Cindy. "I thought you were watching."

Cindy rolled over. The team stood around her, staring. She wanted to disappear. "Yes, I'm fine," she croaked.

After checking for injuries, Barbie let Cindy sit on the bench. The **exhausted** girl was glad to be out of the game for a few minutes. "Gee," Cindy thought, rubbing her sore back, "being the star of the team is painful!"

When Cindy came back into the game, Paulina passed her the ball right away. Cindy passed it right back. "Shoot it yourself!" she told her teammate.

For a moment, Paulina froze in shock. Then she shot the ball. *BAM! SWISH!*

"That's more like it!" Barbie called from the sidelines. "If you have a good shot, don't pass it. Take it yourself."

During a water break, Paulina stormed over to the twin she thought was Jen. "What's up with you?" she demanded.

Debbie was right behind her. "Yeah," she echoed.

Just then, Jen walked over. "What's going on?" she asked her teammates.

Barbie came over to the girls. "Is there a problem?" she asked.

Before Cindy could reply, Paulina answered.

"I don't know how to describe it. Cindy and Jen aren't playing like themselves today."

Cindy started to choke on the water she was drinking.

Jen patted her sister on the back and thought hard. "We were trying to keep it a secret," she said at last. "But I guess we should tell you the truth."

Barbie folded her arms across her chest. "I would like to hear this," she replied.

Cindy gasped. "You're going to tell them?"

"We have no choice," Jen replied. "The truth is," she began, "Jen lost one of her contacts. She can't see a thing."

Cindy let out a deep sigh. "That's right," she added. "And Cindy's been covering for me."

Debbie laughed. "Why didn't you two say something before?"

Cindy smiled at her teammates. "We didn't want to worry you."

Barbie looked at the twins thoughtfully. "I

hope you'll be back to your old selves by the big game," she said.

Cindy and Jen nodded. "Don't worry. We will," they promised together.

Both twins were tired when they got home. They couldn't wait to change back into their normal clothes. They had missed being themselves. But neither twin would admit it to the other one.

After dinner Cindy said to her sister, "I think I'll go out and shoot some baskets. Want to come?"

Jen thought about it and said, "No, thanks. I have some homework I want to finish."

"Wow!" Cindy exclaimed. "I never thought we would be saying that!"

"Me, either," Jen agreed, laughing. "By the way, I may be a little late for Friday's game."

"What?" Cindy cried, grabbing her sister's sleeve. "You can't! Why?"

"I can't tell you," Jen replied. "But it's really important."

"You *are* going to be there, aren't you?" Cindy pleaded.

"Yes. I'll probably just miss the warm-ups," Jen told her. She grabbed her purple, number  eleven jersey out of the **laundry.** "Here, bring my uniform with you. I'll change when I get there," she said. "But don't tell anyone. I don't want the team to panic."

Cindy took her sister's uniform and rubbed her sore back. "If you don't show up, *I'll* panic. This had better be important."

"Why?" Jen asked, grinning. "Was it that hard being me for a day?"

"No!" Cindy said quickly. "It's just that I know how important this game is to you."

Jen touched her sister's shoulder. "I promise I'll be there. I won't let you down, Cindy."

Chapter Five

Finally the big day arrived. Friday afternoon the Gators would play the Puffins for the championship title.

At lunch, Jen was more than just late. She didn't come at all. Cindy wondered if something was wrong.

That afternoon, Cindy waited for all the girls to leave the locker room before entering. Jen was nowhere in sight. Cindy opened her bag and stared at her sister's jersey. "Number eleven," she thought. "That's Barbie's number, too. I'll have to say something to her. But what?"

Suddenly the locker room door opened. Debbie peeked inside. She saw the back of a girl holding up a number eleven jersey. "Hurry up, Jen!" Debbie urged Cindy. "Everybody's waiting for you."

Just then, Cindy had an idea. "I'll be right there," she called, taking off her glasses. She grabbed her contacts out of her bag. After putting them in, she changed into Jen's uniform and ran out onto the court. She wouldn't let her sister down. Cindy would switch with her one last time.

The bleachers were filling up with students and parents. Cindy's parents waved to her in the stands. She waved back and quickly looked away.

During warm-ups, Cindy glanced over at the other team. The players in the yellow jerseys seemed to make every shot they took.

Cindy whispered to Paulina, "Those Puffins look even better than the last time we played them."

Paulina nodded. "Yeah, but we have you, Jen," she replied confidently.

"Great!" Cindy thought. "I just hope our star gets here in time to win this game."

Just then, Coach Curtis arrived. The girls were thrilled and crowded around him, asking questions. But Cindy stayed back. "I wouldn't have missed this game for the world," he told the team. Then he spotted Cindy. "Hi, Jen!" he called.

Cindy smiled and waved. Barbie walked over to her. "Where's your sister?" she asked.

Cindy paused and said, "She's going to be a little late. She had to do something at school. You know her," she laughed, "school first."

Barbie smiled. "I hope she gets here soon," she said. "We need her."

"You're telling me," Cindy muttered.

Back in the locker room, Jen had arrived. In a rush, she threw on a jersey without checking the number. Then she ran out to the gym. But it was too late. The game had already started. And Jen couldn't believe what she saw. *Cindy* was in the game as one of the starting players!

"Oh, no!" Jen cried. "They think she's me!" She sat down on the bench and watched. What she saw made her sad. Cindy's teammates kept passing her the ball. Cindy was trying her best to shoot it, but she kept missing. Soon the score was 26–14. The Puffins were winning.

During a time-out, Barbie noticed Jen on the sidelines. "I'm glad you made it, Cindy," said Barbie. "No glasses today?"

Jen gulped. "Uh, no," she sputtered. "I thought I'd try out these contacts for the game."

"Good idea," Barbie said, smiling.

At the end of the quarter, Cindy staggered off the court. Jen pulled her twin aside. "What are you doing?" Jen demanded.

"I'm trying to cover for you," Cindy replied, still breathing hard. "You said you didn't want the team to panic if you were late."

"Well, I'm back now," Jen sighed. "But I'm

sitting on the bench because they think I'm you. I can't stand it!"

"I know!" Cindy answered. She waved toward the court. "Well, I'm stuck out there because they think I'm you! *I* can't stand it!"

"So let's switch back," Jen suggested.

"We can't," Cindy protested. "We have to wait until halftime. Then we'll change in the locker room. No one will know the difference."

"Okay," Jen agreed.

Just then, Debbie and Paulina came over. "What's wrong now, Jen?" Debbie asked Cindy.

"If you don't start making some baskets, we'll lose this game!" Paulina cried.

"I can't win this game alone," Cindy said.

"That's true," Barbie added. "Remember, we're in this together. No one is more important than anyone else. The team needs each of your strengths to win this game. You can't win by expecting one person to do everything."

Everyone was silent. Then Paulina said, "You're right. Sorry, Jen."

The buzzer sounded, and the teams raced back onto the court.

Debbie was guarding a girl who went up for a shot. Debbie tried to block the ball but hit the girl's arm. The whistle sounded. **Foul**!

"Oh, no!" Coach Curtis exclaimed from the sidelines. "That was her last foul. Debbie's out of the game."

"It's okay," Barbie replied. "The Gators can still do it."

Before the halftime buzzer sounded, the twins sneaked off to the locker room. They wanted to switch jerseys before the others got there.

"I can't believe we fooled them!" Cindy said.

"I know," Jen replied. "I thought Barbie had figured it out when—" She stopped suddenly.

"What's wrong?" Cindy asked.

Jen pointed over her sister's shoulder. Cindy

turned around to see Barbie standing behind her.

"It's all my fault—" Jen began.

"No, it's my fault—" Cindy cut in.

"I think you're both right," Barbie finally said. "Right now you have a lot of explaining to do. And we don't have much time."

Soon the rest of the team arrived in the locker room. The twins told the truth about their switch. Everyone was angry and upset.

Paulina turned to Jen. "We're losing this championship because of you!" she cried.

Jen jumped to her feet. "You can't blame me," she replied. "I can't do everything!"

"It's true," Cindy added. "I've never felt so much pressure to play well as when you thought I was Jen."

"And when you thought I was Cindy," Jen said, "no one passed me the ball."

Cindy added softly, "But I did feel like part of the team out there today."

Barbie cut in. "*I've* noticed that without a 'star' player, everyone seems to work harder. When I put Cindy in, you work more as a team."

"Oh, great," Jen laughed. "Before, everyone was counting on me. Now nobody needs me."

The group laughed.

"We're sorry for putting so much pressure on you," Paulina told Jen.

"And we're sorry for not giving you a chance," another girl said to Cindy.

The rest of the team felt the same way.

The twins smiled. "We're really sorry for tricking you," Cindy said. "We never thought it would hurt anyone."

"But I guess we were wrong," Jen finished. "We'll never do it again."

"You can say that again," Coach Curtis said as he came in. "Your team may forgive you. But the basketball league may not be so understanding."

Cindy's eyes widened. "What do you mean?"

"We may have to **forfeit** this game," the coach declared.

"What?" Jen cried, jumping to her feet. "Just give up and let the Puffins win? But why?"

"Our player list is wrong," he explained. "It states that Jen Martinez is number eleven. And that isn't true. It's against the rules to lie about those things."

"It isn't fair!" Debbie shouted.

"Yeah!" echoed the other girls.

Tears welled up in Cindy's eyes. "We never thought this could happen," she said softly.

Jen cried, "But everyone's worked so hard." Silence filled the locker room.

Just then, Barbie spoke up. "I, too, have a **confession** to make." She held the list of players that she had given to the **officials.**

"I watched the twins all week at practice. I thought

45

that they had switched places. So when I handed in this list, I switched their names back. I put *Cindy* in as number eleven, not Jen."

"All right!" Jen and Cindy yelled together.

The rest of the team cheered, too. Then they formed a huddle. They put one hand in the center of the circle. Barbie looked at the excited faces of the Gators and smiled. "Now let's go **pulverize** those Puffins!" she shouted.

"Yeah!" everyone cheered.

After the huddle broke up, the two coaches pulled the twins aside. "Don't think you're getting out of this so easily!" Coach Curtis began.

"We'll have to tell your parents," Barbie said.

Cindy and Jen nodded sadly. "I guess that's only fair," Jen agreed.

Then Cindy grinned. "But can it wait until after we beat the Puffins?"

The two coaches looked at each other and smiled. "It's a deal," Coach Curtis said.

Chapter Six

The buzzer sounded. Halftime was over. The starting players from each team walked onto the court. Cindy sat on the bench with the rest of the team. But for the first time, she felt as if she really belonged.

From the start of the quarter, the Gators played better than they ever had. Everyone was working together rather than trying to get the ball to Jen. At the end of the third quarter, the score was tied at 40–40.

Barbie looked to Cindy, sitting on the bench. "Do you think you're up to it?" she asked the girl.

"You bet!" Cindy declared.

Having twins on the same team seemed to confuse the Puffins. The girls in yellow could tell that one was a better player. But after the twins had played for a while, one Puffin asked, "Which one's trouble?"

"I can't tell anymore," replied her teammate. "They both look good to me."

Hearing this, Debbie started a cheer on the bench. "Double trouble! Double trouble!"

Cindy couldn't help but smile.

The score was 47–46. The Puffins had a one-point lead. There were thirty seconds left in the game. A girl on the Puffins missed a shot. Paulina ran the ball down to the other end of the court. She stopped to shoot, but two players surrounded her. Paulina passed the ball to Jen.

Ten seconds were left. Jen caught the ball and dribbled it to the basket. But she stumbled. As she fell, Jen saw her sister. She passed the ball to

Cindy with two seconds left.

Cindy bounced the ball, planted her feet, and shot. A Puffin tried to block her but hit Jen's arm instead. *BUZZZZZ!* The ball bounced off the basket. A wave of disappointment filled Cindy.

Suddenly the ref's whistle sounded. Cindy had been fouled! She would get two free throw shots.

Barbie and Coach Curtis called the team together.

"I saw you make those free throws before practice," Barbie reminded Cindy. "If you could do it then, you can do it now."

Cindy wiped her sweaty face and nodded. Then she walked by herself onto the court. She stood at the free throw line. The final buzzer had already sounded the end of the game. So the other players had to watch from the sidelines.

Cindy closed her eyes. She imagined there were no other people in the gym. When the whistle blew, she opened her eyes. The ref handed her the ball. She bounced it two times and shot. *BAM! SWISH!* The score was tied.

"Yeah!" Cindy heard her sister shout from the sidelines. Her teammates cheered.

Cindy closed her eyes again. When the whistle blew, she bounced the ball two times and shot. *SWISH!* The Gators won the game!

Girls in purple flooded the court, cheering and hugging. Barbie and Coach Curtis were thrilled, too. Then the players and coaches formed a line to congratulate the other team.

After everything was over, the twins caught Barbie on her way out. "Barbie," Cindy called, "how did you know we switched places?"

Barbie chuckled. "It wasn't hard. I hate to break it to you, but you aren't very good actors."

"You mean you didn't fall for my 'new

contacts' story?" Jen asked.

The three basketball players laughed.

"But why didn't you say anything?" Cindy asked.

"You needed to work it out yourselves," Barbie replied. "That's usually the best way to learn."

Jen sighed. "I guess we have to face Mom and Dad now," she said.

"Yeah," Cindy agreed. "We'll probably get punished."

Jen nodded. "But I guess we deserve it."

"By the way, Jen," Barbie asked, "why were you late to the game?"

"Oh, I almost forgot!" Jen exclaimed. She dug through her backpack and pulled out some papers. She handed them to her sister.

Cindy stared at the neatly typed paper. "What's this?" she asked. Then she read out loud, "'A True Champion, by Cindy Martinez.'" She shook her head. "I don't understand. I didn't write this."

"No. I did, for the school newspaper," Jen said. The grin on her face spread from ear to ear. "After I got you that *D* in English, I asked Mrs. Kirk what I could do to fix it. She said that I could write an article for the newspaper. She'll use it as extra credit." Then she added shyly, "Mrs. Kirk seemed to think it was pretty good, too."

Cindy beamed. "You did this for me?"

Jen thought for a moment. "Yes, at first," she replied. "But now I know we'll have to tell Mrs. Kirk the truth on Monday. I did find out, though, that I really like writing—when it's about basketball. I may even join the paper as a sportswriter."

Barbie smiled. "That's great, Jen. And when Cindy's a pro basketball player, you can interview her."

Cindy laughed. "Now *that* would be a switch!"